THIS WALKER BOOK BELONGS TO:

For Timothy

First published 1985 by
Walker Books Ltd, Walker House
87 Vauxhall Walk, London SE11 5HJ

This edition published 1988

© 1985 Philippe Dupasquier

Printed in Spain by Cayfosa, Barcelona

British Library Cataloguing in Publication Data
Dupasquier, Philippe
Robert the great.
I. Title
843'.914[J]   PZ7
ISBN 0-7445-1061-9

RBERT
the Great

PHILIPPE DUPASQUIER

WALKER BOOKS
LONDON

Robert lived with his mother and father
in a big house. He had no brothers or

sisters but he had lots of toys to play
with. One day...

...his mother came into his room. 'Robert,' she said, 'be a little angel and run down to the shop for some biscuits. Aunt Susie is coming to tea.'

On the way Robert met Mrs French.
'Going shopping for your mummy?' she said.
'What a good little boy you are!'
At the flower stall the lady said, 'That's Mrs
Waters' little Robert. Isn't he a little darling?'

Mr Brown in the shop said, 'Hello,
little man. What can I do for you?'
'Little again!' Robert thought crossly.
'Why do they all say I'm little?'

When Robert got home Aunt Susie was there.
'You little sweetie, my favourite biscuits!' she
cooed. 'Here, help yourself, my pet. I know what
hungry tummies little boys like you always have.'
'I am *not* little!' Robert screamed furiously and he
marched up to his room and slammed the door.

From that moment on, Robert was a different
boy. He was always staring into the mirror.
'What rubbish,' he'd say. 'I'm not little. I'm *not*.'

He sulked. He did all kinds of silly things, trying to make himself look bigger.

Robert's behaviour got worse and worse.
His parents were at their wits' end.

They tried everything. In the end
they sent for the doctor. But that was
no good. Robert bit him.

That night he dressed up as a horrible monster.

'I'm a giant. I'm going to gobble you all up!' he shouted.

'This can't go on,' said Mr Waters. 'What that boy
needs is a change.'
So the next day they went on a trip to the zoo.
Robert was as horrid as ever. 'I hate zoos,' he said.

He hated the parrots; he hated the
giraffes; he didn't even like the monkeys.
Then a great big truck came into the zoo.
On the truck was a cage and in the cage
was an enormous tiger.

The keeper got up to check the bolts.
'Keep back,' he warned. 'This fellow eats people for breakfast.'
Just then a terrible thing happened. The tiger jumped at the cage door. The keeper fell over backwards. The door flew open.

The tiger leapt out. People were
screaming and running everywhere.

But Robert was left behind. He was standing in front of the cage. All by himself. Except for the tiger.

The tiger crouched, ready to spring. Someone
screamed, 'It's going to eat the little boy!'
But Robert had seen the open cage.
The tiger pounced; Robert dashed inside.
The tiger was right behind him.

But before the tiger could reach him Robert
squeezed out through the bars on the other
side. No sooner had his feet touched the

ground than he quickly ran round the truck.
SLAM! He had the cage door shut and bolted.
The tiger was trapped.

The crowd couldn't believe it. Everyone
cheered. Robert was a hero! They carried
him round the zoo in triumph.

Next time he went shopping nobody called
Robert little.

'My, what a big boy you are,' Mrs French
called as he passed.
'Stronger than a tiger,' said the lady at the
flower stall.
Everyone he met seemed to know about his
great adventure.

'Here comes Robert the Great. Aren't we all proud of our big boy then?' said Aunt Susie the next time she came to tea.

'I'm not really big,' Robert said, 'or I couldn't have got through the bars of the cage, could I, Aunt Susie?'

The End